Join
Super Soccer Boy
online:

www.supersoccerboy.com

⚽ Fun activities
⚽ Football facts and quiz
⚽ All the latest on the books

And much more!

SUPER SOCCER BOY

AND THE SNOT MONSTERS

BY JUDY BROWN

Piccadilly Press • London

First published in 2010 by
Piccadilly Press Ltd, 5 Castle Road, London NW1 8PR
www.piccadillypress.co.uk

Text and illustration copyright © Judy Brown, 2010

ISBN: 978 1 84812 083 9

1 3 5 7 9 10 8 6 4 2

Printed in the UK by CPI Bookmarque, Croydon, CR0 4TD
Cover design by Simon Davis
Cover illustration by Judy Brown
Text design by Simon Davis

Mixed Sources
Product group from well-managed
forests and other controlled sources
www.fsc.org Cert no. TT-COC-002227
© 1996 Forest Stewardship Council
FSC

Chapter One

Vile Virus

'*AAACHOO!*' sneezed Mrs Gribble as Harry walked into the kitchen. He darted quickly to his right as a small globule of snot flew past, missing his ear by millimetres before colliding with the kitchen cabinet.

'Oh, I'm so sorry, Harry,' sniffed his mum, dashing over to wipe away the offending blob. 'This cold is awful. I'b so snotty ad I just can't stop sneezing. *A . . . AAA . . . AAACHOO!*' This time she made sure she caught the sneeze in a tissue.

'*AAACHOO!*' came a much louder, but lower sounding, boom of a sneeze from upstairs. The glasses in the cupboard rattled.

'Dad's got it too, then,' Harry said.

'Yes, I'b afraid so,' replied his mum. 'Although being a man, his is much worse, of course.'

They weren't the only ones who were ill – it seemed that half of Middletown had a cold and it was spreading fast.

Harry wondered if his super soccer powers had made him immune to it, though. His mum said the virus probably wasn't fast enough to catch him! Harry couldn't actually remember being ill since the day he was transformed by the lightning strike – the day he went from being 'Harry Gribble who couldn't even dribble', to a boy with super soccer skills.

'Go back to bed, Mum, I can do my own packed lunch,' Harry said considerately. Well, he wasn't actually being that considerate – if his mum kept on sneezing like that, he didn't know what might end up in his sandwich.

'You are a good boy, Harry.' His mum looked at him with bleary, red-rimmed eyes and yawned. 'I feel like I could sleep for a week. Have a good day at school,' she mumbled, shuffling out of the kitchen.

Harry got a cereal bowl out of the cupboard and turned on the TV.

'I wonder what's happening in the world today, Ron,' he said, handing his pet rat a tiny bowl of Coco Pops.

'*AAACHOO!*' sneezed the newsreader. 'I'm so sorry. Excuse me.' She blew her nose. 'As I was saying, the cold epidemic continues to spread. There is now officially a national shortage of tissues and many supermarkets have completely sold out. Schools are insisting that pupils bring in their own supplies after many found that all their toilet rolls had been used instead.

'There was uproar yesterday when the F.A. Cup replay had to be abandoned because neither team could stop sneezing.'

'Did you hear that, Ron?' said Harry, spraying Coco Pops all over the table. 'This is getting really serious.' He looked at the kitchen clock. 'Oops! Better get on with making my lunch or I'll be late.'

Chapter Two

School's Out

Harry made himself some tuna, Marmite, mayonnaise and pickled-onion sandwiches and put them in his lunchbox along with a carrot, a banana and a Yorkie biscuit. Then he trotted off to meet Jake at the corner of Crumbly Drive.

For the first time in ages, Harry got there before Jake. He soon realised why – Jake had a cold. He was plodding along the road with a red nose, bleary eyes and a box of man-size tissues under his arm.

'Bordig,' mumbled Jake, when he reached Harry.

'Poo!' said Harry. 'What's that pong?'

'It's Nan's menthol vapour rub. It's s'posed to help me breathe.'

'You sound awful! How do you feel?' asked Harry.

'Lousy,' said Jake. 'I wasn't too bad when I got up, but now ...*A* ... *A* ...*AAACHOO!*

Jake's mega sneeze went straight through Harry's brain. 'I feel like poo.'

'Why don't you go home?' asked Harry.

'Forgot my key. Mum and Dad at work. [*Sniff.*] Anyway, Mum says it's only a cold and you can't be off school unless you have a temperature. I can't wait for lunchtime – colds always make me hungry.'

Harry smiled. Jake was just *always* hungry.

School was crammed full of sneezing people. Obviously it wasn't only Jake's parents who thought that having a cold was no reason to stay off school. Harry felt sorry for them but it was driving him nuts – if it hadn't been for his super soccer reactions he would have been sneezed on several times.

The first lesson was physics.

'Good . . . *AAACHOO!* . . . morning, class,' said Mr Turner, the physics teacher. 'Today, I thought . . .' (He paused to blow his nose.) '. . . we could measure the velocity of our sneezes!' He was great like that, Mr Turner — he always came up with fun ideas.

They tested everyone's sneezes one by one. It was all brilliant fun but rather messy. In the end, Raj's sneeze won by four-and-a-half miles per hour. Mr Turner gave him a Mars Bar as a prize.

At breaktime in the canteen, it was a nightmare. People were squabbling over tissues, spilling things in mid-sneeze and falling asleep at the tables. A Year Two who'd run out of tissues sneezed so hard that he left a pool of slimy snot on the floor. Another Year Two, who hadn't noticed, skidded across the floor and knocked over a huge bin of snotty tissues. Nobody felt much like picking them up.

After break, Harry's class was supposed to have games with Mr Blunt. This was the lesson Harry looked forward to more than any other, but when they got to the changing room, there was a note pinned on the door.

ALL LESSONS CANCELLED TODAY.

GO TO LIBRARY TO STUDY.

There was a suspicious looking green stain on the corner of the paper, as if someone had sneezed on it and tried to wipe it off.

When they got to the library, it was packed full of students. It seemed that all the teachers had had the same idea.

After lunch, the headteacher called a special assembly. Harry was not pleased. They were supposed to be doing football practice for a game next week – not that the rest of the school team felt much like playing.

'Quiet, please!' said the Head, before blowing his nose hard into a particularly large and nasty-looking handkerchief. 'I'b afraid I hab no choice but to close the school early today. Since toborrow is Friday, I'b decided that everybody should stay at hobe till Bonday. Any pupil who needs to may stay in the library till hobe tibe.'

SNIFF SNIFF

I'M SO SLEEPY.

AACHOOO!

Harry was expecting a big cheer – there would have been one normally. It seemed, though, that everybody was too busy sneezing, blowing their noses or just generally feeling too ill to care.

The Head blabbed on for another ten  minutes about how it wasn't a holiday, how they should all do their work, etc, etc, and then they were sent home.

'Do you want to come back with me?' Harry asked Jake, remembering that Jake had forgotten his key. 'We could have a kick-about in the park on the way.'

'OK,' said Jake between sniffs.

They walked back past the park, but Jake was

obviously in no mood for football. Harry suggested Jake sat on the bench while he tore around at super speed, practising his dribbling skills. He could hear Jake sneezing from the other side of the park and decided he'd better get him home.

'Don't you think it's strange that so many people have this cold?' Harry asked.

'Why?' sniffed Jake. 'People are always catching colds from each another.'

'But not like this,' said Harry. 'Not everybody, and not all at the same time. It's a bit freaky.'

'If ... *AAACHOO!* ... you say so,' groaned Jake.

They turned the corner into the High Street.

'Look at that!' said Harry suddenly. He pointed at a huge advertising hoarding, up on the wall near the supermarket. 'At least someone's trying to cure the cold.'

Chapter Three

Germ of an Idea

That evening in Harry's house it was very quiet. Apart from the sound of sneezing and nose blowing, that was.

All his family had a big bowl of chicken and vegetable soup for supper – exactly the kind of food people feel like when they're coldy. His little sister Daisy fell asleep in hers. Ron sat on Harry's lap, waiting for scraps as usual.

'I'm so tired,' said Mum, wiping a combination of soup and snot from Daisy's face. 'Me too,' yawned Dad. 'I'm going to wash up, watch the news and go to bed. No work tomorrow – everybody's ill.'

'No school either,' said Harry, feeling a little worried. 'What if everyone gets sick? How will things keep going?'

'It *is* a bit of a worry,' agreed Mum.

They sat in the living room and turned on the TV while Daisy snored quietly on a beanbag.

'Good evening . . . *AAACHOO!* . . . Excuse me . . . and welcome. Tonight on the news – as the cold crisis spreads and local services struggle to cope, we talk to Professor Mucus about the growing epidemic and his attempts to find a cure.'

Harry looked at the TV as the camera turned to a strange-looking man with wild, mad-scientist hair. It was the same man that he and Jake had seen on the advertisement.

'Professor, what can you tell us . . .  AAACHOO! . . . about this awful epidemic?' The newsreader sneezed an enormous sneeze into a big spotted handkerchief.

'Well, what we are experiencing, Simon, is an extremely contagious form of head cold or "rhinovirus".'

Harry smiled as he got a mental picture of a rhino with a cold. How messy would that be?

'It seems to be spreading unusually fast, however, and infecting everyone who comes into contact with it. Not only that, but it is very long lasting.'

'Yes, yes,' Simon the newsreader said, nodding. Harry could see that he had long since stopped listening and was finding it hard to keep his eyes open.

'You see, Simon,' Professor Mucus continued loudly, making him jump, 'I have been researching the common cold nearly all my working life. As a child, I suffered terribly from cols. Did you know that the average child may get anything between six and twelve colds a year? My record was fifteen.'

'Fascinating!' said Simon, doing his best to stay focused. 'And now?'

'Ah, I haven't had a cold for nearly twenty years. I'm trying to find . . .' (Professor Mucus paused for a micro-second, and Harry noticed a very slight twitch at the corners of his mouth, as if he was trying his best not to smile.) '. . . a cure. If anybody who has a cold would like to contact me, they can become part of my research programme. There is a telephone number you can ring if you would like to join my crusade against the common cold and rid the world of this nuisance once and for all. Every day I am getting closer to my goal, I assure you!'

'And what will happen to ... [*Sniff!*] ... those who ring?'

'I'm glad you asked me that, Simon.' Professor Mucus continued, his eyes twinkling. 'They will be given the location of a meeting point near to their home, then they will be collected by coach and taken to my research facility. Once there we will do a mucus extraction which will give temporary relief, and the mucus we collect will be

used for experiments. Collections are due to start tomorrow.'

'Eeeeeeewwwww! He's going to suck everyone's snot out,' said Harry, wincing.

'Shush, Harry,' said Dad. 'We're trying to listen.'

'I also hope to have mobile collection units running soon, which will be able to detect a sneeze within a five-mile radius. And, being mobile units, they will be much more convenient for the general public.' Professor Mucus smiled smugly.

'Tell me, Professor,' said Simon the newsreader, getting out a clean handkerchief, 'you don't seem to have this cold. Is there any reason for that, do you think?'

'My only explanation is that because of my

prolonged contact with the rhinovirus as a child and during my research, I have presumably developed a kind of immunity. Since I was about twenty, I have been very lucky. I can't actually remember the last time I even had a runny nose. Ha! Ha! Ha!'

'That's amazing,' Simon said enviously. 'Professor, thank you for coming in. And here . . . *AAACHOO!* . . . is that number, for any of you who would like to take part in the research.'

The phone number appeared on the screen and flashed for maximum effect.

'Write that down for us, Harry,' said Mum. 'I might give them a call tomorrow.'

'He said everybody who came into contact with the virus caught it – but *he* hasn't got it. I know he says he's developed an immunity but it all seems a bit odd to me,' said Harry as he scribbled down the number. Then he went on quietly, 'I smell a rat – no offence, Ron.'

Suddenly he had an idea. 'I'm sure Jake could do with a mucus extraction, Ron – he's got so much of it – and I could have a snoop around.'

Harry picked up the phone and started to dial.

Chapter Four

The Mad Professor

Meanwhile; several miles away in his secret underground laboratory, Professor Mucus prepared another canister of his special 'Rhinovirus Release Spray'.

'Tee hee hee!' he chuckled to himself.

'Another few cans of these spread about and absolutely everyone will be infected. The fools don't even realise that I'm the reason they're all sneezing! Soon they'll all be nose-dripping idiots and I will have my revenge! They will be helpless before me, their MASTER!!! Mwahahahaha!'

Professor Mucus leaned back in his chair and closed his eyes. His thoughts drifted back to his schooldays. They were not happy times for Malcolm Mucus.

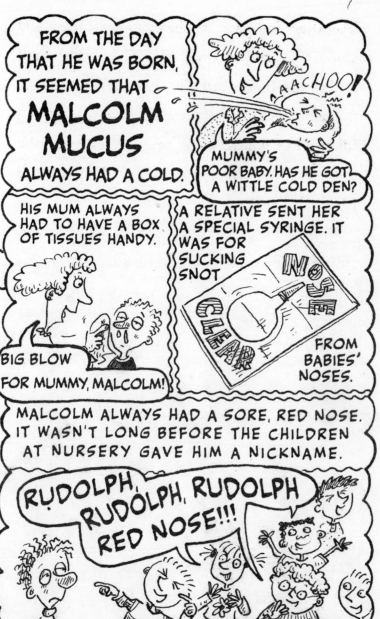

FROM THE DAY THAT HE WAS BORN, IT SEEMED THAT **MALCOLM MUCUS** ALWAYS HAD A COLD.

AAACHOO!

MUMMY'S POOR BABY. HAS HE GOT A WITTLE COLD DEN?

HIS MUM ALWAYS HAD TO HAVE A BOX OF TISSUES HANDY.

A RELATIVE SENT HER A SPECIAL SYRINGE. IT WAS FOR SUCKING SNOT

NOSE CLEAR

FROM BABIES' NOSES.

BIG BLOW FOR MUMMY, MALCOLM!

MALCOLM ALWAYS HAD A SORE, RED NOSE. IT WASN'T LONG BEFORE THE CHILDREN AT NURSERY GAVE HIM A NICKNAME.

RUDOLPH, RUDOLPH, RUDOLPH RED NOSE!!!

29

POOR MALCOLM

NOT A GOOD NAME TO HAVE BY THE WAY IF YOUR NOSE IS ALWAYS BLOCKED.

THEY SAW COUNTLESS DOCTORS.

HE MIGHT JUST GROW OUT OF IT!

BUT NONE OF THEM COULD HELP.

THINGS GOT WORSE AFTER HE STARTED SCHOOL.

ER SORRY, I'VE BROKEN MY LEG!

FOOTBALL ANYONE?

MOST OF THE CHILDREN DIDN'T WANT TO PLAY WITH HIM IN CASE THEY CAUGHT HIS COLD.

OTHERS WERE JUST PLAIN NASTY!

BEAT IT, SNOT FACE!

HI, GUYS!

THE NAMES THEY CALLED HIM WERE FAR WORSE THAN THOSE AT NURSERY.

BOGEY FACE!

SNOT BOY!

SNIFFY!

PHLEGM FACE!

BOGEY BOY!

SUPER SNOT!

HIS SURNAME DIDN'T HELP MUCH EITHER.

AT SECONDARY SCHOOL, IT BECAME VERY CLEAR THAT DESPITE HIS CONSTANT SNIFFING MALCOLM WAS EXCEPTIONALLY BRIGHT.

REPORT CARD
ENGLISH A*
MATHS A*
SCIENCE A*
HISTORY A*
GEOGRAPHY A*

PROUD GLOW!

HE LOVED SCIENCE.

101 EXPERIMENTS FOR BRAINIACS

WOW! THANKS MUM AND DAD!

HAPPY BIRTHDAY, MALCOLM!!

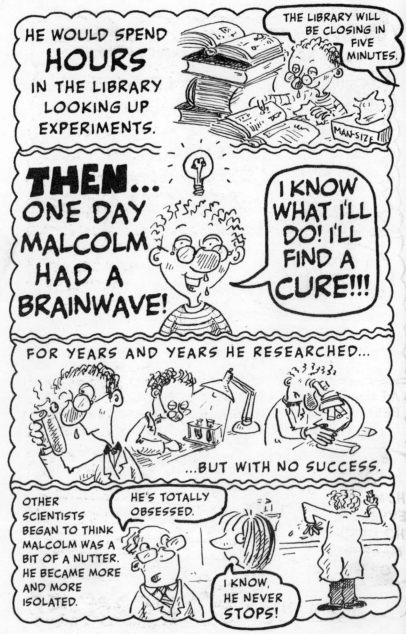

BUT... AS MALCOLM GOT OLDER, HE GOT FEWER AND FEWER COLDS.

IT SEEMED HIS YEARS OF SUFFERING AS A YOUNGSTER MEANT THAT HE HAD DEVELOPED A KIND OF **RESISTANCE!**

I CAN BREATHE!

NOW HE WASN'T SUFFERING ANY MORE, HE CARED LESS AND LESS ABOUT A CURE.

AS HIS HEAD CLEARED OF THE MUCUS THAT HAD BEEN FILLING IT FOR YEARS, MALCOLM REALISED THERE WAS SOMETHING ELSE HE WANTED...

IF ONLY I COULD HUMILIATE EVERYONE HO USED TO MAKE FUN OF ME!

AND EVERYONE ELSE AS WELL!

...HE WANTED **REVENGE!**

33

Professor Mucus opened his eyes and stared at the door, which led to the rest of his research facility. He smiled evilly to himself.

'And now for Stage Two of Operation Mucus.'

Chapter Five

Snot Funny

It took a while to get through because the line was busy, but when Harry eventually got to speak to someone at Professor Mucus's research facility, he booked Jake in for a mucus extraction.

'Sounds absolutely disgusting,' said Jake, when Harry told him about it.

'Go on, it'll be fun!' said Harry.

'Fud! Fuddy idea of fud you've got!' said Jake through a very blocked nose. 'Still, it would be dice to be able to breathe agaid for a bit.'

So, the next morning, Jake, Harry and Ron waited in the High Street with a whole load of snotty, bleary-eyed people to be collected by coach and taken to Professor Mucus's research facility. The coach arrived pretty much on time, and they all climbed on board.

There were complimentary tissues for everyone and there was an information film all about cold viruses playing on a screen at the front of the coach. After a few minutes, though, most of the cold-filled people nodded off. The film was followed by a short, guided video tour of the research building, presented by Professor Mucus himself.

'This,' he said proudly, 'is our extraction chamber.' Harry watched as the camera panned over the rows of chairs, and the tubes coming in and out of them, and decided that it was probably a very good thing that Jake had dropped off to sleep.

After about an hour, the coach pulled up outside a large, white, shiny building in the middle of nowhere.

'Stay out of sight, Ron,' said Harry as they got off the coach. 'I don't think anyone would be very happy if they saw you, and research labs are no places for rats.'

The coach party was led through the entrance to a large waiting room, just as another coach-load was being led out. This snot-free group of people was smiling and laughing, happy to be able to breathe again for a while. Jake cheered up as soon as he saw them, and so did everyone else.

'I can't wait to be able to breathe properly,' said Jake. 'I wonder how long it will last.' They sat down and spotted a door in the corner of the waiting room. It said *EXTRACTION CHAMBER* in large letters and above it were two lights, one red and one green. The red one was lit. Moments later it went off and the green light came on, and Jake felt a twinge of nerves.

Professor Mucus entered the room. He was tiny!

'Welcome, welcome! Thank you so much for coming. The extraction process takes about fifteen minutes to complete and is quite

harmless although you may feel a little discomfort.'

Jake's stomach did a weird flip.

'If you should decide not to go ahead, you may just observe, but I assure you that the extraction will give you at least three hours' relief from a blocked or runny nose. Now, if you would all like to follow me into the extraction chamber, we can begin.'

As Harry had seen in the film, the extraction chamber was full of chairs. Every chair had a mask attached to it, and tubes led from the mask into a glass container behind the chair, which had a sort of plunger in it. The snot donors each chose a chair and sat down.

'My assistants will come around and fit the suction masks, and when everyone is ready we will begin,' said Professor Mucus. 'After fifteen minutes the suction will stop automatically. You will then be taken to the refreshment room for tea, coffee or juice and a biscuit.'

Jake, hungry as usual, wondered if he would be allowed two.

Chapter Six

The Snot Plot

While Professor Mucus's assistants moved from one chair to another, fitting the masks to the slightly nervous-looking roomful of snot-filled people, Harry slipped off to one side.

When all the masks were in place, the Professor went over to a large control panel, pressed a sequence of buttons, and the machines came to life.

'Just relax,' he said. 'You will soon begin to feel some suction.'

The plungers in the tanks began to move up and down and a strange expression appeared on Jake's face – in fact, everyone's faces. It was a cross between surprise and disbelief.

The tanks began to fill with nasty green snot of various shades and runniness. It was truly disgusting.

'It's a good thing they can't see what's coming out,' Harry whispered to Ron, feeling a little queasy himself. He noticed that there were pipes

coming out of the snot tanks and it was being pumped somewhere else. 'Let's see where it's going, Ron.'

Harry traced the pipes around the room with his eyes. They seemed to pass through the wall. He sneaked along the wall behind the chairs and tried the door at the end. It wasn't locked, but one of Professor Mucus's assistants was nearby. If

he opened the door she'd be bound to notice. Then, for a second, she turned to check one of the tanks. Quick as a flash, Harry opened the door and slipped through.

He was stunned at what he saw.

'What the . . .?'

The pipes that came through from the extraction chamber ran along the ceiling and into an enormous glass tank. It was the size of a swimming pool and it was full of disgusting, bubbling snot.

'What on earth would anyone collect a swimming pool full of snot? Why does he want it all?' Reluctantly, Harry went over for a closer look. 'Surely Professor Mucus wouldn't need that much snot for his experiments, and what's the point of mixing it all together?'

He walked down the side of the tank and poked his head around the corner.

There were taps coming out of the bottom of the tank, attached to hoses leading into what looked like huge jelly moulds. There were five of them altogether. At the top of the door to each of the moulds was a small glass window and at the back there were power leads that disappeared into the wall.

'I wonder what those are for?' puzzled Harry. 'This is getting really weird.'

Slightly nervously, Harry opened the door to one of the jelly moulds. 'Yuk!'

There was a puddle of semi-dried snot on the floor, and little bits of dried bogey stuck to the inside of the door. It smelled pretty nasty too.

Suddenly, Harry's super hearing detected someone coming.

He had to hide! He looked around desperately, but there was nowhere else he could go. Grudgingly, he stepped inside the jelly mould and pulled the door *almost* closed behind him. (He certainly didn't want to get stuck.) Something dripped on his head. He didn't want to think about what it was. 'Yuk, yuk and triple

yuk! This is so gross, Ron!'

Professor Mucus entered the room. He strode over to the jelly moulds and looked up at the tank. Harry, peering through the crack in the door, noticed that there were measurements on the side of the tank. The green muck in the tank wasn't that far from the mark that said *Maximum*.

'Ooooh! Not far now. Almost there! There's nearly enough to carry out my plan. We just have to make sure everybody keeps catching my specially-designed cold and producing my super snot.'

Harry thought to begin with that Professor Mucus was talking to himself, but then he realised that he was actually talking to a figure just to the side of the moulds. He tried to see who it was, but there was no way he was able to without giving himself away. All he could make out was a vague shadow.

'We can get in a few more coach-loads today, and tomorrow I'll send out the mobile collection units. Then our army can march! Mwahahahahahaha!'

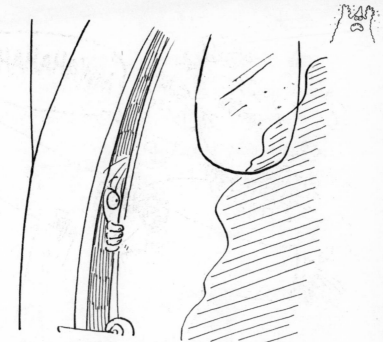

'Army?' thought Harry, 'What *is* he on about?'

'Tonight, though, I want a couple of you to plant some more of my rhinovirus release canisters. There are none at the shopping centres yet and we have to maintain the infection. Wait at least an hour after it closes so that you're not spotted.'

Just then, a bell began to ring.

'Aha!' said Professor Mucus. 'That will be the end of the session. Go back to the lab – you mustn't be seen.'

The shadow moved away, and Professor Mucus headed back to the extraction chamber.

'So Professor Mucus is behind the whole epidemic!' said Harry. 'This looks bad, Ron, very bad. This is a job for Super Soccer Boy!'

Chapter Seven

Snot Free

Harry whizzed at super soccer speed back to the extraction chamber, creeping in just as Professor Mucus's assistants began to remove the masks.

'Wow!' said Jake, without even a hint of a snotty nose. 'That was amazing. I thought it was going to suck my brains out!'

All of the people in the room were now free of snot. They were breathing in and out deeply, with expressions of absolute joy on their faces, and, even though they knew it was only going to last a few hours, they were laughing and chatting happily.

'If you would like to follow my assistant, Mr Minchin, he will take you to the refreshment room,' Professor Mucus announced.

Harry pulled Jake to one side as they were all herded towards the canteen. 'You won't believe what I just heard!' he said.

'What is it, Harry? You look really stressed,' Jake said happily.

'Professor Mucus – he's the one that's been infecting everyone. He's engineered some sort of super-cold.'

'What on earth would he do that for?' said Jake. 'It's crazy. You must have got it wrong.'

'No way, he said it himself. I promise you, he's well dodgy,' Harry went on. 'He's collecting a huge tank of everyone's snot to use for some sort of plan.'

Jake looked at him. 'D'you know how barmy that sounds? What on earth would you do with a tank full of snot?'

WHAT ON EARTH WOULD YOU DO WITH A TANK FULL OF SNOT?

'Well, obviously, if I knew that, I'd know what the plan was. All I'm sure of is that he's up to no good.

That's definite.' Harry was beginning to get

cross. 'I can prove it tonight if you come to the shopping centre with me.'

'All right, all right, keep your hair on, I'll come.' Jake felt so much better right then that he would have agreed to anything, even bungee jumping.

They had their juice and biscuits – Jake was allowed as many biscuits as he liked. While they sat in the canteen, Harry looked out of the window. He could see the new mobile extraction units being prepared outside. It made him wonder how much time there was until Professor Mucus had as much snot as he needed. Not much, he suspected.

'Are you OK, Harry?' asked Jake as they travelled back on the coach. 'You're very quiet.'

'I'm OK,' answered Harry glumly. 'How about you?'

'Right now,' Jake said, 'I feel fantastic! Maybe my cold is gone for good!'

'Fat chance,' said Harry.

Back in his secret laboratory, Professor Mucus updated his experiment log with details of the day's collection. He closed it and put it back on a bookshelf, which was crammed with many more similar looking books.

'Twenty years' hard work,' Professor Mucus said. 'I've come so far!' He smiled to himself and pondered how much he had changed since he first began his research.

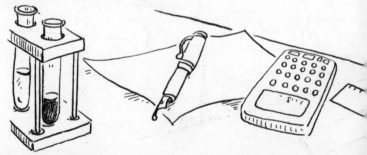

65

Professor Mucus turned as he heard someone approach. 'Ah, it's you,' he said. A large green mountainous thing stood beside him. It looked like a humungous bogey. 'Are you ready for tonight's little task?'

The large, green bogey thing nodded slowly. 'RAAAAR!' it said, opening its cavernous green mouth.

'Excellent!' declared Professor Mucus. 'You know what to do – just make sure you're not spotted.'

The giant living bogey turned and left.

Chapter Eight

S'not Very Nice

An hour after dinner, Jake, still happily snot free, cycled round to Harry's house.

'Hi, Jake,' said Harry, opening the door. 'Mum, I'm just going to Jake's for a bit. Won't be long.'

'Make sure you have your phone and your key,' said Mum. 'I'b going to bed early – my cold's still dreadful.'

'*AAACHOO!*'
sneezed Daisy as she
poked her head
round the door to say
hello to Jake. She
sneezed on his jeans
instead and giggled
guiltily.

'OK, Mum,' said
Harry.

They walked to
the shopping centre
at the end of the
High Street, Ron
riding along in
Harry's hood. The

roads and streets were deserted. Perhaps everyone
was tucked up in bed, blowing their noses.

'You still OK?' Harry asked.

'So far,' said Jake. 'Although I'm beginning to
feel a bit of a tingle in my nose as if a sneeze

were coming. What is it we're looking for, anyway?'

'I'm not entirely sure,' said Harry. 'I just know that they're going to plant some of the canisters that Professor Mucus has been using, to spread his super-cold at the shopping centre,' he explained.

'Oh, OK. Do we know when though?' asked Jake.

''Fraid not, but he did say something about going at least an hour after closing.'

69

'Hope it's not too long. I'll be toast if I stay out too late.'

They went into an alleyway behind the shopping centre where the recycling bins were kept and waited nervously.

'I reckon they'll try and get in this way.' Harry pointed to a door marked *Goods Entrance*. 'All we have to do is wait.'

They were lucky (well, sort of) – they didn't have to wait long.

Two dark shapes appeared at the end of the alley.

'It looks as though they've arrived,' said Harry, excitedly. As the shapes moved into the light, the boys were speechless.

Two large green snot monsters stood in the alley, looking around them. They were semi-see-through, they glistened slightly under the streetlights, and little crusty bits came off them as they moved. One was carrying a small metal canister.

'Oh . . . my . . . God!' Jake whispered hoarsely. 'Please tell me I'm having a nightmare.'

'Stay very still. I don't think we want them to spot us,' said Harry.

'Funnily enough, I wasn't thinking of introducing myself,' said Jake, all the colour draining from his face.

A stray cat had also seen the monsters. Pretty stupidly, it ran into the middle of the alleyway, fur fluffed up. It wasn't remotely scary – even Ron was unimpressed. Then it began hissing at the snot monsters. This was not a good move.

The slightly lighter coloured monster moved towards it. Frozen in terror, the cat stayed rooted to the spot and the snot monster sort of rolled over it. When the monster had passed over and the cat reappeared, it had been turned into a little green snot statue of a cat, dripping slightly.

'I think I'm going to be sick.' Jake clamped his hand over his mouth.

'Shhhh!' said Harry, not feeling too great himself.

For once in his life, Ron found himself feeling sorry for a cat.

The other snot monster, meanwhile, was putting the canister of super-cold right by the air conditioning vent for the shopping centre.

'So that's why it's spreading so fast,' said Harry. 'Very clever!'

Then everything started to go a bit wrong.

'*AAACHOO!*' sneezed Jake.

'Uh oh!' said Harry.

The snot monsters turned and saw Harry and Jake hiding at the back of the alley. Harry looked behind him. It was a dead end – there was nowhere to escape.

The snot monsters opened their cavernous

OOPS!

mouths and made a sort of gurgling, roaring sound. Their foul breath came towards Harry and Jake in clouds. It was really disgusting.

The boys looked at each other, trying not to panic.

RURGLE!

Harry scanned the alley for anything useful.
There were empty cardboard boxes, random bits
of rubbish, an old sock, a broken shopping
trolley – the usual kind of junk you find in an
alley. Ron jumped out of Harry's pocket to see
if he could find anything else. In desperation,

Harry started kicking whatever he could see at the monsters.

'I'll try and distract them,' Harry called out, 'so you can make a run for it!'

'It's not working,' yelled Jake.

He was right – the little bits and pieces just bounced off or stuck to the snot monsters, making them even angrier.

'I need something with more oomph!' shouted Harry.

Out of the corner of his eye, Harry spotted Ron jumping up and down, trying to get his attention. There was a crate of dented tins from the supermarket, tucked behind the recycling bins. Harry sped over and scooped up an armful.

'Be ready to run for it, Jake. These should do the trick.'

Harry booted the tins at one of the snot monsters.

For a moment, the monster faltered as the tins lodged themselves in its body.

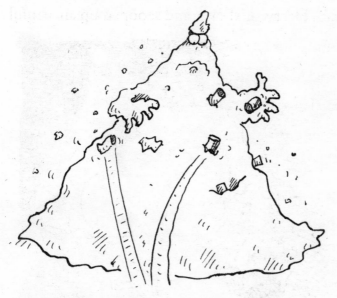

'Yay!' cheered Jake, but not for long.

As they watched, the monster picked the tins out one by one and fired them straight back at Harry. It was all he could do to dodge them. Not only that, but it was firing lumps of snot at him too. The hollows that the tins had made in the monster's body closed up, leaving no trace and seemingly no damage at all.

The monsters were now right in front of Jake, who had resigned himself to his fate. But then something strange happened. The monsters swerved away from him and headed straight for Harry instead. Seeing that Jake had a chance to get away, Harry shouted, 'Run for it, Jake, I'll meet you at home!' At least he hoped he would.

But Jake wouldn't leave without Harry.

He ran to the open end of the alley and waited.

The snot monsters were advancing towards Harry and were just metres away. There was only one thing for it – Harry scooped Ron up and shoved him in his jacket, put his head down and, with a burst of super speed, he ran straight for

the nearest snot monster. At the last moment, he swerved to one side, squeezing between the monster and the wall of the alley. Well, nearly. In fact, his super soccer speed seemed to take him clean through the edges of the monster's body. Harry didn't stop, but carried on until he got to the end of the alley, grabbed Jake and ran, at as fast as he could, all the way home, leaving the surprised-looking monsters far behind.

WHOOSH

'Yuk, yuk and triple YUK!' said Harry when he eventually came to a stop, outside his house.

'You're all covered in . . . snot!' said Jake, with a look of disgust.

'Tell me about it!' groaned Harry. Bits of bogey were beginning to go crusty and drop

off. 'It feels so gross. I am going to have a *very* long shower.'

'Did I really see what I thought I saw?' asked Jake.

'Yep!' said Harry, feeling stickier by the second.

'Remind me never to doubt you again,' said Jake.

Harry smiled. 'I wonder why they didn't go for you.'

'Dunno. Maybe because I wasn't the one attacking them with rubbish.'

'Hmmm, maybe,' pondered Harry. 'Anyway, I have to get this stuff off – it's revolting.'

'*AAACHOO!*' sneezed Jake.

'Sounds like your cold's back,' said Harry, sympathetically. 'You'd better go home. I'll ring you in the morning so we can work out what to do.'

'Night, Harry. Enjoy your shower.'

Harry did.

Chapter Nine

Super Snot Boy

Harry woke with a start. He'd had a dream where snot monsters were turning everyone into snot statues like the cat in the alley and Professor Mucus was taking over the world. Harry knew he had to act fast.

Harry still wondered why the snot monsters hadn't gone for Jake. He also wondered how Jake was feeling today.

'Please tell be it was all a bad dreab,' Jake said when he answered the phone.

''Fraid not,' said Harry. 'You're all bunged up again then?'

'Yes, it's worse than before. I've beed blowig by dose all bordig.'

'Well then, how about another trip to Professor Mucus's snot extraction chamber? I could do a bit more snooping.'

'D'you really think it's safe, after last dight?' asked Jake nervously.

'What else can we do? No one in their right mind would believe us if we told them what we saw,' Harry replied.

There was a pause. 'Good point,' Jake agreed eventually.

'And I want a sample of that snot to test,' Harry added.

While Harry was waiting for Jake in the High Street, he saw one of Professor Mucus's mobile extraction units.

ACHOO!

MOBILE COLLECTION UNIT

sneeze and we're there

one sneeze and we're there

A woman coming out of the sports shop sneezed and, before she knew what was happening, two of the Professor's assistants, dressed in white coats, jumped out of the van, clamped a mask on her face and started sucking out the contents of her nose. She looked rather surprised, to say the least.

Harry smelled the now familiar smell of menthol vapour rub and realised Jake was

standing behind him.

'I don't think it will be long before Professor Mucus has exactly what he needs,' said Harry gloomily. 'You know what he meant when he talked about an army now, don't you?'

Jake knew.

They boarded the coach. Jake got out a little pot of menthol vapour rub and dabbed some on the end of his sore red nose. There were sticky bits of the stuff on the outside of the pot, he'd opened and closed it so many times.

'Does that stuff help?' asked Harry. 'It really pongs.'

'A bit,' said Jake. 'My nan swears by it.' The smell wafted in Harry's direction and he winced. So did Ron.

'I wonder . . .' Harry said thoughtfully. 'Can I borrow it for a bit?'

'S'pose so,' said Jake. 'What for?'

'Just something I'd like to try out,' Harry said.

Soon they were at Professor Mucus's research facility and, as before, they were taken to the extraction chamber. Once again, Harry crept behind the seats as the masks were being fitted.

The machines hummed into life and Harry darted super fast to the door at the end of the room and opened it. 'OK, Ron, time for a bit more nosing around.'

The first thing that Harry did was to check the tank. It was very close to the *Maximum* mark now.

'Looks like he's nearly ready to move, Ron.'
He went over to one of the big jelly mould
things. 'These must be what he uses to make the
monsters.'

He opened one of the doors, took out a
spoon from his pocket, scooped up some of the
goo that lay on the floor and put it into a small
plastic container.

Then he walked around the back of the
moulds. 'What's here I wonder?' he said.

He found a metal staircase and Harry peered down. It was an amazing sight – there was a room filled with snot monsters! The Professor's assistants seemed to be working on experiments – they were obviously in on the whole plan. Some were filling super-cold canisters, others were on

computers. The monsters were all just like the ones he and Jake had met the night before.

Then Harry spotted five more monster moulds.

'Oh my God!' said Harry. 'An army of those and we're in big trouble, Ron.'

He leaned over a little further to get a better look. As he did so, Jake's pot of menthol vapour rub fell out of his pocket and bounced noisily down the stairs into the room below.

'Oops!' said Harry under his breath. 'That wasn't supposed to happen!'

Before Harry could stop him, Ron ran after the pot.

'No, Ron,' said Harry remembering what had happened to the cat before. But it was too late – Ron had already got to the bottom of the stairs.

Ron picked up the pot and looked up. He was surrounded by snot monsters. One of them bent down towards him and Ron held the pot in front of him in self defence. For a moment the monster hesitated, screwing up its face in disgust and Ron grabbed his chance to escape.

'I thought so!' Harry whispered. 'They don't like the smell. That's why they didn't go for Jake.'

Harry waited anxiously for Ron to get back and watched the snot monsters to see if they would follow. It seemed that they didn't think it was worth chasing after a rat, especially not a smelly one.

'Phew! That was close. It's a good job none of the assistants saw you – otherwise we'd have been in real trouble.'

Ron's whiskers twitched.

BRRING!

'That's the bell for the end of the suction session. We'd better get back to Jake,' said Harry.

Chapter Ten

The Snot Plot Thickens

Jake was once again feeling great.

'It's so nice to be able to breathe,' he told Harry. 'You've no idea.'

Professor Mucus waved to the current coach party as they left for their refreshments. He looked again when he saw Jake and Harry.

'Those boys were here yesterday,' he said to his assistant, Minchin. 'And that one didn't have suction either time.' He pointed at Harry. He added suspiciously, 'Find out who he is.'

'Right away, Professor.'

Meanwhile, Harry was telling Jake what he'd seen. 'You wouldn't believe it!'

'Funnily enough, for once I probably would,' said Jake.

'There's a whole room full of snot monsters back there. There's something else as well – we found out why they didn't go for you in the alley.'

Jake looked surprised.

'It's this smelly stuff,' Harry explained holding up the pot of menthol vapour rub. 'They don't like it.'

'Wow! Well, it's easy, then. All we have to do is cover everyone in vapour rub.'

'I don't think it's that simple. It only meant that they went for me first. If there was an army of them, I doubt they'd be so choosy. But it's a start, at least.'

'I guess so.' Jake sounded disappointed. 'What shall we do then?'

'Good question. Whatever we do, we'd better do it quickly. It looks like Professor Mucus has all the snot he needs.'

It was true. At that very moment, Professor Mucus was talking to his snot monsters.

'All right, my lovelies, time to start assembling an army!'

Just then, Minchin dashed in. 'Professor, we may have a problem. I've found out who that boy is!'

Professor Mucus, his finger poised over a big red button, turned around. 'What are you talking about?' he said, irritated at the interruption.

'It's Harry Gribble . . . they call him Super Soccer Boy.'

Professor Mucus paused, thinking. He had

heard some stories about a football-obsessed boy.
'I wouldn't worry about some little show-off.
Nothing will stand up to my creations!'

'But, Professor –'

'Enough!' shouted Professor Mucus. Then he
thought for a moment. 'Wait, do we know
where this boy lives?'

'Yes, I have his address here,' said Minchin.

'Well, in that case, I know exactly where we
can start our campaign. Mwahahahaha!'

Professor Mucus pressed the big red button. The moulds began to fill with snot from the tank. At the same time, another tube carrying Professor Mucus's special cocktail of chemicals, the mixture he'd spent fifteen years perfecting, was also pumped in. It all took about three minutes.

When the moulds were full, they started to vibrate, just a little to begin with but, as the power to them increased, the vibrations grew stronger and stronger and louder and louder, until ... *PING!* A timer went off and the process was complete.

The door latches released automatically and out stepped ten brand new snot monsters, yawning and stretching like newborn babies, and giving off sparks of static electricity.

'Ten down, ninety more to go. Mwahahahah! By morning my army will be ready to march!'

Meanwhile, Harry and Jake were at Harry's house, discussing their next move.

'I'm going to do some work on this sample I collected, to see if I can come up with any ideas,' said Harry. 'In the meantime, I think it would be a good idea to get hold of as much of this stuff as we can.' He held up the pot of menthol vapour rub.

'I can go to the chemist on the way home,' Jake agreed. 'I've only got a few quid, though.'

'Here,' said Harry, handing him his football-shaped moneybox. 'There's some money in there. Just get as much as you can.'

'Better go before the shops shut,' said Jake. 'I'll be round first thing in the morning.'

Harry saw him out, then went back to his

room and looked at the container of snot he'd collected earlier.

'OK, Ron, let's see what we have.'

He took off the lid and gasped. The blob of snot was moving.

'Now for some real testing!' said Harry.

Harry set up his digital camera so he could film what he was doing to show Jake the next day. Then he put the blob on a tray on his desk. It bounced up and down angrily.

Harry took out a cotton bud and coated it with some of the menthol vapour rub. 'Now let's see . . .'

Harry waved the cotton
bud in front of the blob. At
first, it shrank away,

but after a few minutes
it just seemed to get
angrier.

Then he tried actually
poking the angry blob. A
hole appeared. 'Hmmm
interesting,' he said.

The hole didn't close up.
He poked it a few more
times. More holes appeared.

He poked it again.
It quivered, wobbled
about for a second,
then just lay

AHA!

motionless on the desk. 'Aha!' said Harry.

Chapter Eleven

Snot Attack

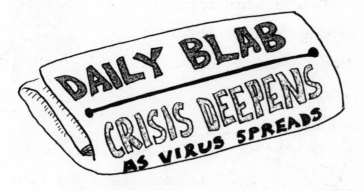

Harry woke early. Everyone else was still in bed when he zoomed down for breakfast. The newspaper on the doormat made gloomy reading, but Harry knew there could be worse to come. He was longing for Jake to arrive so he could tell him what he'd found out. He didn't have to wait long.

Ding dong.

Harry went to open the door.

'Morning, Jake,' said Harry, chirpily.

'Bordig,' said Jake. He was snotty again.

Jake handed Harry a bag. It had eight pots of menthol vapour rub of various brands inside.

'It was all I could get,' he said.

'Cool! But there's something else we're going to need. Let me show you what I found out last night.'

Harry's words were drowned by an enormous uproar outside.

All they could hear was people shouting and screaming and the sounds of police cars, fire engines and ambulances.

'What on earth is going on out there?' croaked Dad from upstairs. 'Some people are trying to sleep.'

Harry and Jake looked at each other.

'Stay inside,' Harry called to his parents. They peered over the landing, looked at his expression and decided to follow his advice.

Harry and Jake went outside. At the end of Crumbly Drive, there were seven snot monsters. They were advancing down the road, smothering anyone that got in their way. As they did, suckers came out of their bodies and drained the victims' snotty noses before encasing them in a hard crusty coating of snot. The street was scattered with snot statues whose wild staring eyes watched helplessly.

Mum, Dad and Daisy were standing at the bedroom window, watching in total disbelief.

Behind the snot monsters there followed a TV news crew, keeping a safe distance but filming the drama as it unfolded.

'It's incredible,' said the reporter. 'These monsters seem to be made from, well, what I can only describe as snot.'

Jake ran to the end of the garden path.

'No, Jake, don't get too close!' yelled Harry, pulling him back.

'They won't come near me, though – they don't like how I smell.'

'No, that's what I was about to tell you – the smell isn't enough. Come inside and I'll show you what I mean.'

Harry ran upstairs and Jake followed. He showed Jake the remains of the snot he'd been testing.

'The snot I brought home yesterday was still moving. I got it from one of Professor Mucus's monster moulds. I guess it must have come off one of the snot monsters. I tried wafting the menthol smell at it, but in the end it just made it angry.'

'We're stuffed then,' said Jake, alarmed.

'No, we're not! Look!' Harry showed him the video of last night's experiments. Jake gazed open-mouthed.

'Wow!' said Jake. 'But we'll never be able to get close enough to poke those giant ones.'

'No. So we need to do it from a distance.'

'But that didn't work when we were in the alley.' Jake was confused.

'Not then it didn't, but if we hit them with something covered in the menthol vapour rub...'

Jake understood instantly. 'So we need something we can fire at them ...'

'Footballs!' they said together.

They grabbed the pots of menthol vapour rub, ran downstairs and into the back garden.

'There are five footballs out here and Daisy

has a couple of balls too, but we're going to need more.'

Harry quickly began to smother the balls they'd collected with menthol vapour rub, while Jake frantically started texting.

'What are you doing?' asked Harry, thinking it was an odd time to start sending texts.

'The football team,' said Jake. 'They'll all have at least one football.'

'Brilliant!'

In the living room, Daisy was watching a TV newsflash of what was going on outside. Harry's mum and dad were staring out of the window in horror.

'Our house, our house,' said Daisy, bouncing up and down. 'It's famous!'

'These monsters seem to have appeared from nowhere!' said the reporter. 'No one knows . . . but what's this . . . who is . . . it's . . . it's . . . Professor Mucus!'

Professor Mucus was riding high on the shoulder of a snot monster. He was carrying a megaphone.

'Mwahahahaha!' bellowed Professor Mucus. 'Bow at my feet, you feeble, snivelling little creatures,' he sneered to the people in the street, who were frozen in terror. 'Bow to your master!'

'He's mad!' cried Mrs Gribble.

'Clearly,' said the reporter, 'Professor Mucus has taken leave of his senses. It looks like we're doomed.'

The next thing Daisy saw as she watched was a bit of a surprise. Her brother and his friend appeared on the TV, carrying lots of balls.

Chapter Twelve

Holey Snot

Professor Mucus and the snot monsters had passed Harry's house and were heading for the other end of Crumbly Drive. By now, the street was full of snot statues. Everybody else had fled inside any available house and anxious faces were at all the windows. The TV news crew was still filming the action but trying to keep themselves safe at the same time.

Harry and Jake ran into the street. Ron tried to follow but Harry made him stay inside – it was too dangerous.

'Hey, you! Bogey faces!' shouted Harry at the back row of snot monsters. 'Oi! I'm talking to you!'

'What's this?' said the reporter excitedly. 'It looks like, yes, it is! It's Super Soccer Boy!'

Harry lined up the footballs across the road.

'Come and get me, if you think you're hard enough!' he taunted.

Meanwhile, Jake ran over to the reporter and grabbed the microphone.

'We need footballs, or any sort of ball you can find,' he shouted urgently. 'Bring them here. We need to cover them in menthol vapour rub . . . so bring that t—'

The reporter grabbed the microphone back.

'Er, thank you,

young man, I don't think this is any time for silly jokes,' she sneered, holding the microphone out of Jake's reach.

'Just watch Super Soccer Boy – you'll see what I mean!' Jake yelled.

The back row of snot monsters had turned and was heading for Harry. He was ready for action.

The monster in the middle opened its great gooey green gob and roared at him. Little bits of bogey shot out and landed in the road. There was a collective 'Eeewwwww!' from everyone watching.

POW! Harry kicked the first of the footballs, right into the monster's mouth. It went straight through and came out the other side, hitting another one of the monsters as it passed.

'GOOOAAALLLLLLAAAA!' shouted Harry.

He booted again. The shot was so powerful, it

went straight through the snot monster's hand, bounced off the lamppost behind and shot back through its shoulder. The monster stared in dismay at the holes that had appeared in its body.

Boof! BOOF! Harry booted two more.

One of them got the monster right between the eyes and it sank to the ground. There was a huge muffled cheer from the houses, and one from the TV crew.

'I've only got two balls left, Jake! Here goes!' Daisy's bunny ball and a spotty one she'd won at a fair went through another monster.

'We need more balls!' said Jake to anyone who was listening.

The reporter suddenly took notice of what Jake was saying. She turned to the camera. 'You heard the boy,' she said. 'We need balls, and fast!'

'Don't forget the menthol vapour rub,' said Jake.

'Oh, er, yes, and, er, menthol vapour rub!'

Suddenly, windows in the street began to open and balls of all shapes and sizes were thrown towards them.

'Quick, cover them in the vapour rub!' Harry shouted as he whizzed around picking them up.

Jake, with the help of some of the TV crew, worked as fast as he could and, one by one, they

lined the balls up for Harry. The snot monsters advanced towards him angrily. Just as they reached him, he let go another barrage. Two more of the monsters were peppered with holes and sank to the ground. There was another cheer. It was much louder this time because all the windows were open.

Professor Mucus turned around to see what was going on. 'NOOOOOO!' he screamed when he saw that three of his precious monsters had been destroyed. 'I'll get you, you little squirt, you won't defeat me! There are loads more snot monsters in my army, and they're all on their way!'

Now Harry was in big trouble. He only had

a few tennis balls, a rugby ball and a couple of beach balls left, and he wasn't going to be able to get those to go very far.

'We need more ammunition!' shouted the reporter hysterically to the camera. 'GET FOOTBALLS AND MENTHOL VAPOUR RUB!!!'

The rest of the snot monsters advanced on Harry. He managed to find a couple of balls that had bounced back towards him. But then things got even worse. Professor Mucus had summoned the rest of his army and the street was soon crammed full of snot monsters. And they were all out to get Harry.

Suddenly, a van screeched to a halt behind him, and then another. The TV appeal had worked! Both vans were full of balls from the local sports centre. A man in a white coat from the chemist in the High Street was running up to them, clutching a big box full of pots of

menthol vapour rub. More and more people came to lend a hand smothering the footballs.

'It's a wonderful sight, viewers, truly wonderful,' said the reporter, tears in her eyes. 'The whole community is coming together to defeat this menace.'

Soon, more than a hundred balls were ready and the helpers formed a chain to pass them to Harry.

BOOF! BOOF! BOOF! One by one, Harry launched the balls at the snot monsters and, one by one, they withered and collapsed.

But Harry was beginning to get tired. 'I don't know how much longer I can keep this up for,' he said. His legs were aching and the fumes from the vapour rub were making him feel dizzy.

'Don't worry, Harry, we're here to help.'

Harry turned to see his entire Little League team ready for action. The snot monsters didn't stand a chance!

'Blast you, Super Soccer Boy!' screamed Professor Mucus. Then he started to cry like a baby. 'Boo hoo hoo,' he sobbed. 'It was such a perfect plan. *AAACHOO!* Oh no, now I've got a cold! It's not fair!'

As the last of the snot monsters collapsed to the ground and melted, the frozen bogey statues melted too, released from the monsters' evil grip – although they were still covered in nasty green goo. And in an alleyway behind the shopping centre, a rather confused cat yawned and stretched.

THAT WAS A LONG NAP. WHAT'S ALL THIS STICKY STUFF?

STRETCH

Chapter Thirteen
Final Score

Moments later, the police arrived and dragged the sobbing, sneezing Professor off to the police station.

'I haven't had a cold for twenty years, s'not fair. Why have I got one now?' wept Professor Mucus as they led him away. '*AAA . . . AAA . . . AAACHOOOOO!!!*'

'Maybe it's the shock of defeat!' said Harry, laughing.

The fire brigade were busy washing the remains of the snot monsters off the street, while Jake was enjoying his fifteen minutes of fame. He was telling the whole story to the reporter from start to finish and she was listening intently to every word.

Harry, on the other hand, was being paraded around the street on the shoulders of his team mates. The whole street was clapping and cheering. His mum and dad were very proud.

THREE CHEERS FOR SUPER SOCCER BOY!

Over the next few weeks things returned to normal. Football practice got back on schedule and the school team came top of the league. It was all thanks to Super Soccer Boy, of course.

HARRY'S F⚽⚽TBALL FACTS!

Aberdeen were the first team in Britain to have a dug out.

Depending on the size of the person...

The first world cup final was held in 1930 in Montevideo, Uruguay

20 red cards were shown in one match in Paraguay in 1993

In 1950, India withdrew from the world cup because Fifa wouldn't let them play barefoot!

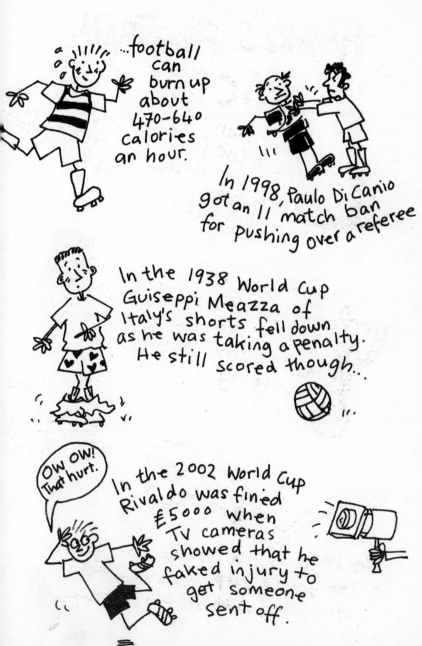

...football can burn up about 470-640 calories an hour.

In 1998, Paulo Di Canio got an 11 match ban for pushing over a referee

In the 1938 World Cup Guiseppi Meazza of Italy's shorts fell down as he was taking a penalty. He still scored though...

OW OW! That hurt.

In the 2002 World Cup Rivaldo was fined £5000 when TV cameras showed that he faked injury to get someone sent off.

Coming soon . . .

Super Soccer Boy and the Attack of the Giant Slugs

A chemical spill turns hundreds of slugs into giants bent on revenge. How is Harry ever going to stop the slimy maniacs?